*Colin T*

# I'M A
# DINOSAUR

# *Illustrated by John Richardson*

## STRAW HAT

First published in 1993 by Straw Hat

Text copyright © Colin Tulloch 1993
Illustrations copyright © John Richardson 1993

**British Library Cataloguing in Publication Data**
Tulloch, Colin
> Help! I'm a Dinosaur
> 1. Title   II. John Richardson
> 823'.914 (J)

Cover design by Expressive Design • Yeovil
Printed and bound in Great Britain by W.B.C. • Bridgend
for the publishers Straw Hat • Cambridge

ISBN 0-9520571-3-1 (Cased)
ISBN 0-9520571-4-X (Limp)

# CONTENTS

# Chapter One

## Dinosaur in Store

Crispin Todd had found something
### ≧ FASCINATING. ≦
Crispin was in the toy department of
Glossidges. His mum was busy buying a
present for his cousin Amanda who was
in hospital having her squint seen to.
And while waiting for her, Crispin had
found **THIS AMAZING THING...**

It was a marvel of electronic wizardry,

the very latest in toys.

NEW! DINOS
BE A DINO

Exhib nc wc
aue a
v

All you had to do was
get in, zip up and be **A DINOSAUR** and

**TERRIFY EVERYBODY.**

Crispin sidled towards the dinosaur suit.

**WAS**
      **MUM**
            **WATCHING?**

3

No. Mum was busy sighing over things
for Amanda she couldn't afford. Like
the shop with working lights and cash
till. She was having a little play with it
while she thought no-one was looking.

**What about the assistants?**

No. They were busy, too. They were
attending to a Very Important Customer,
the Hon. Mrs Burton-Bradstock.

Mrs Burton-Bradstock wanted a doll's
pram and, like any self-respecting
Honourable, she believed in value for money.

Mum remembered she was a grown-up.

Amanda would have loved this but it's much too expensive. I'll ask an assistant to find me a nice painting set.

But the assistants were still busy.

Excuse me...

This really is the biggest cheapest pram we have, Mrs Burton-Bradstock.

What a ridiculously expensive little thing, please keep looking

£1·99

Since Mum couldn't make herself heard she decided she'd better see what Crispin was up to.

Crispy, where are you?

6

# The dinosaur twitched.

7

# Chapter Two

## Groans, Slobbers and Shrieks

Mum pulled from the outside. Crispin
pulled from the inside.

**STILL** the assistants were busy.

I suppose I must accept this tiny expensive pram but I'm sure Harrods would have found me a bigger and cheaper one. In future I shall take my custom there.

This threw the assistants into a panic again.

Will someone please listen to me. My son is trapped inside a dinosaur suit. I cannot answer for the consequences if he is not released soon!

Crispin was getting **cross**.

When Glossidges are selling faulty goods they ought to do something about it. Isn't there something called a 'Citizens' Charter'? I'm a citizen.

9

And off he shambled, learning the controls as he went.

He'd pressed the **GROAN** and **SLURP** buttons by accident.

In Ladies' Fashions they didn't notice the groaning and slurping coming closer because they were holding a show. It was the big event of the year.

GROANNN
SLAVER
SLOBBER
SHRIEK

Crispin was now slavering and slobbering, having pressed the **SLAVER** and **SLOBBER** controls.

12

The only person not to flee was the
Chief Fashion Buyer. She was frozen
with fear.

# Chapter Three

## Mum very Crossaurus in Glossidges Staurus

Crispin set off. Noisily through Soft
Furnishings -

14

Electrifyingly through Electricals…

Where his
electronics
jammed all the TV sets.

On the escalator,

him.

from

away

escalated

people

SCREAM

UP

# Mum was still trying to get attention.

Mum ran back to the other end of the toy department.

# Chapter Four

## Crispin T Rex!

In a panic, Mum raced around Glossidges looking for Crispin.

Since that didn't sound very tempting --

Crispin continued on his way. Through the Eaterie where nobody wanted to eat any more…

…and Blankets and Bedding where people dived for cover.

21

The only person on the Third Floor who didn't know there was a dinosaur about was the girl in Customer Services. This was because she was eating an apple and listening to pop music through earphones.

23

At which Crispin became annoyed. One cannot blame him. Service for dinosaurs is shocking. In his annoyance he pressed

# BLOOD-CURDLING SCREECH

He said something like…

…though the printed word cannot hope to convey the horror of that cry. But the expression on the girl's face gives you a hint. Look at the way her hair is both frizzling and standing on end at the same time.

The music no longer interests her. Her foot has stopped tapping.

She wasn't any good. Crispin went off
to look for someone more useful.

The Manager, perhaps.

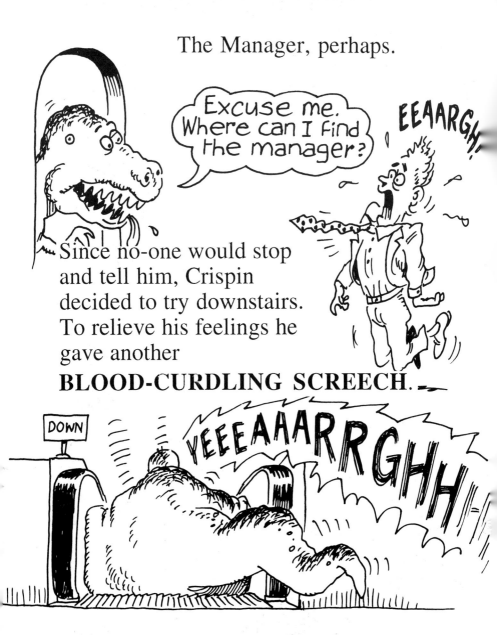

Since no-one would stop
and tell him, Crispin
decided to try downstairs.
To relieve his feelings he
gave another
**BLOOD-CURDLING SCREECH.**

Just as Mum was arriving on the Third
Floor and inquiring after the dinosaur's
whereabouts.

# Chapter Five

In his Ground Floor office, the Manager had heard the noise.

29

Fearlessly, in the finest tradition of Glossidges, the Manager raced up the escalator. He was particularly fearless because he was one of the few people in the store who knew it was not a real dinosaur.

He knew that it must be the new pride and joy of the toy department.

And he was particularly speedy because
of the sound of breaking glass. Crispin
was having a smashing time.

Mum heard the noise and ran. So now there were two very angry people racing towards Crispin.
Who would get there first?

We'll probably have to sell our house to pay for this. Come here Crispin. I want to withdraw your privileges so very, very **badly**.

**Would it be Mum?**

**Or the Manager?**

I shall be laughed at by all the other managers **they've** never had all their customers chased out by a toy. You'll pay for this, you, you **monster**.

Probably the Manager would have got
there first if a lady pushing a very large,
very cheap doll's pram hadn't been
crossing the top of the escalator. Mrs
Burton-Bradstock was the only person
in Glossidges who didn't know there
was a dinosaur about. She was too busy.

It was an unfortunate moment to cross
Crispin's path. His rage was at its
greatest. It was the moment he chose to
release all his weapons at once.

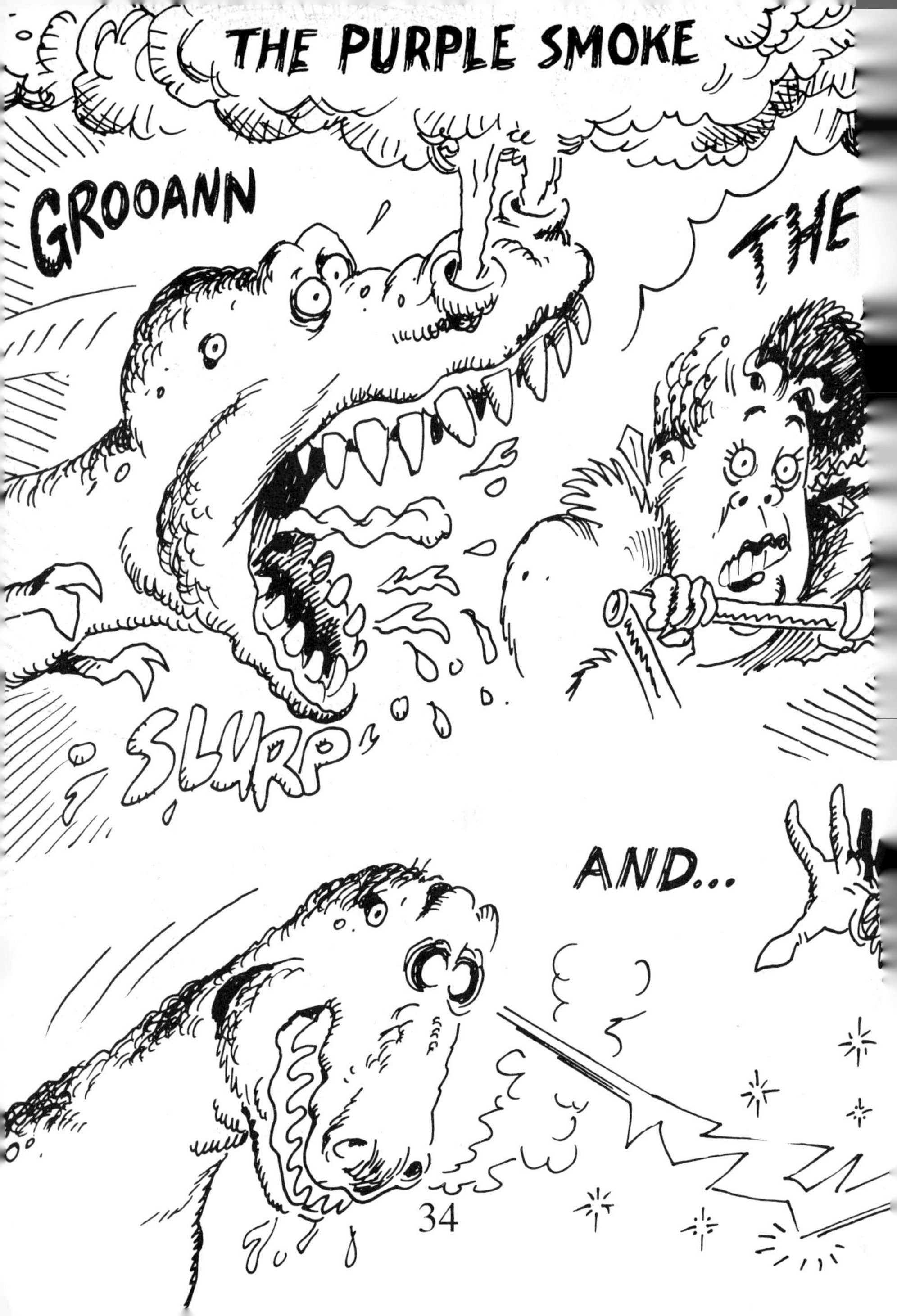
THE PURPLE SMOKE
GROOANN
THE
SLURP
AND...

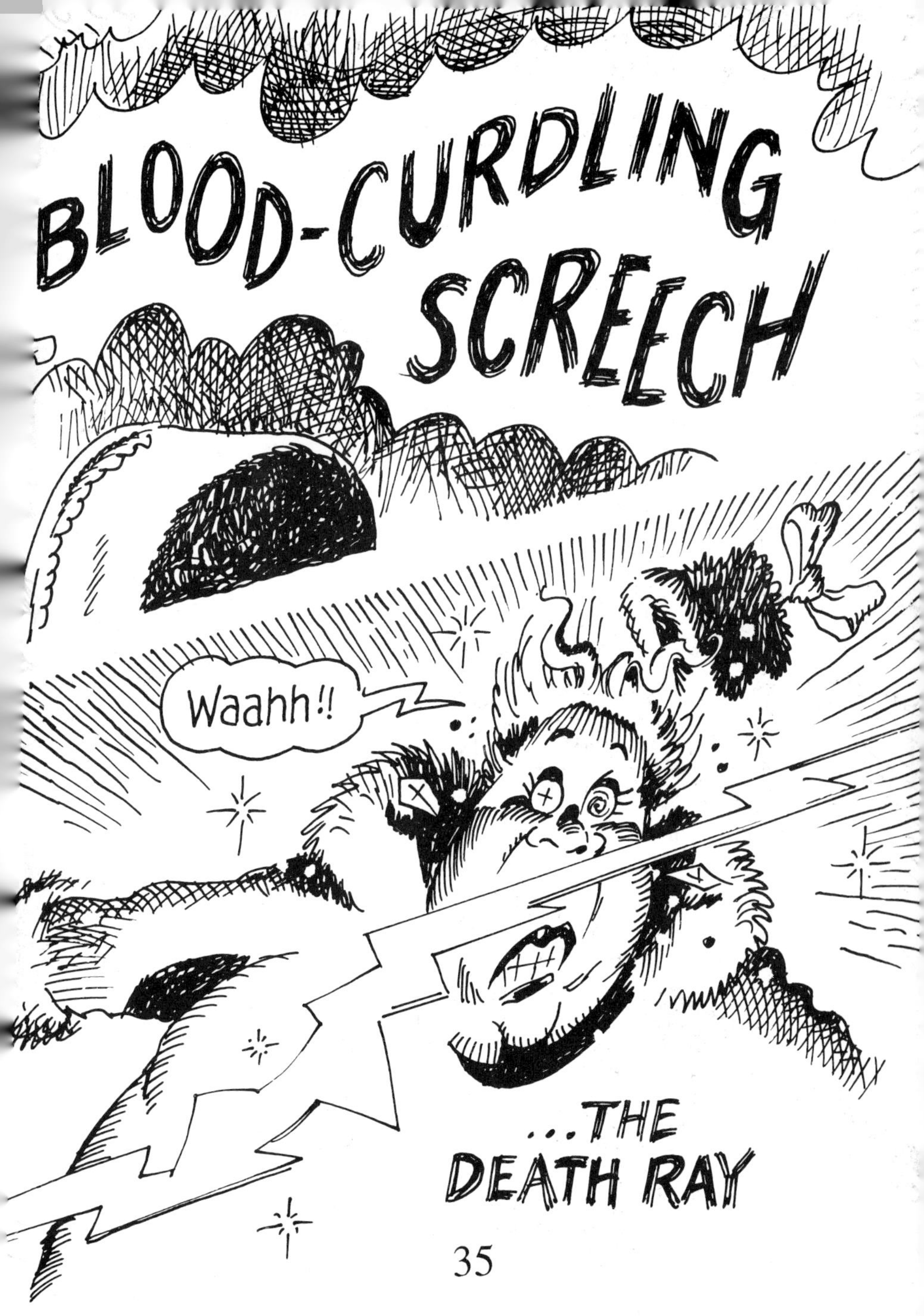
BLOOD-CURDLING SCREECH
Waahh!!
...THE DEATH RAY

...and dumped them there.

You grace Glossidges with your very presence. I would not have had this happen for a **MILLION POUNDS**.

**Mum was terrified by those expensive words.**

I want to withdraw your privileges so very **VERY** much.

38

# Chapter Six

## Dino-hero

But…what was this? The Manager had trodden on something.

No wonder she'd wanted a **BIG** pram.

40

The Manager suddenly became human.

Crispin was suddenly a very popular dinosaur. With his own hands and pliers from the Do-It-Yourself department, the Manager unstuck the zip.

Crispin the hero! The Manager offered him any toy he wanted.

Now that he was out of it the dinosaur suit looked

FASCINATING

again.

But the battery-powered police car with flashing lights was pretty good, too.

And Mum was thrilled with her free toy.

She'd be giving it to Amanda, of course.

# The End